P9-DCO-493

TESSA KRAILING

The Petsitters Club

2. The Cat Burglar

Illustrated by Jan Lewis

BARRON'S

First edition for the United States, Canada, and the Philippines
published by Barron's Educational Series, Inc., 1998.

Text Copyright © Tessa Krailing, 1997
Illustrations Copyright © Jan Lewis, 1997

All rights reserved.

First published in Great Britain in 1997 by Scholastic Children's
Books, Commonswealth House, 1-19 New Oxford Street, London
WC1A 1NU, UK
A division of Scholastic Ltd

No part of this book may be reproduced in any form, by photostat,
microfilm, xerography, or any other means, or incorporated into any
information retrieval system, electronic or mechanical, without the
written permission of the copyright owner.

All inquiries should be addressed to:

Barron's Educational Series, Inc.
250 Wireless Boulevard
Hauppauge, New York 11788
http://www.barronseduc.com

ISBN 0-7641-0570-1
Library of Congress Catalog Card No. 97-38858

Library of Congress Cataloging-in-Publication Data
Krailing, Tessa, 1935-
     The Petsitters Club. 2, The cat burglar / Tessa Krailing.—1st ed.
        p. cm.
     Summary: When Sam and the other members of the Petsitters Club
agree to guard Mrs. Makepeace's cat from a cat burglar, they find
themselves in the middle of a family feud.
     ISBN 0-7641-0570-1
     [1. Clubs—Fiction. 2. Cats—Fiction.] I. Title.
PZ7.K85855Pe   1998
[Fic]—dc21   97-38858
                                                            CIP
                                                            AC

Printed in the United States of America
9 8 7 6 5 4 3

Chapter 1

Up a Tree

Sam was walking home from the store when she heard a man's voice calling, "Here, kitty. Here, kitty, kitty. Kitty, come down."

She stopped and looked over the wall. On the other side was a big old house surrounded by a large garden. The garden appeared to be empty, but then she heard the man call again.

"Here, kitty. Here, kitty, kitty. Kitty, *please* come down!"

She looked in the direction of the voice. A thin man dressed in black crouched in the bushes, staring up into a tree.

Suddenly he seemed to lose patience. "Oh, come down, you stupid cat!"

Sam leaned over the wall. "Do you want some help?" she asked.

The man jumped as if she had frightened him. "What?" he snapped rudely.

"I said, do you want some help? Only I'm an expert, you see."

"An expert in what?" he demanded, even more rudely. "Cats—or tree-climbing!"

"Cats. Well, any kind of pet, really. My friends and I, we belong to a Petsitters Club, so we're used to taking care of animals."

The man didn't look at all impressed. If anything he looked more impatient than ever.

Sam added, "I'm not a bad tree-climber, either."

He stared at her thoughtfully. "Could you climb up this tree?"

"I think so." She climbed over the wall and went closer. "How high is the cat?"

He pointed up. On a branch about five feet off the ground sat a smoky-gray cat with pointed ears and golden eyes. It gazed haughtily down at Sam and swished its tail.

"Oh, how beautiful!" Sam exclaimed.

"It's called a Burmese," said the man. "Think you can reach it? I'd climb up myself, but I've got a touch of rheumatism."

7

"I can reach it okay," said Sam. "It's not very high. In fact, I'd have thought it could easily get down by itself."

"I bet it could," said the man. "But it won't."

Sam stared up at the cat. The cat closed its eyes and opened them again in a slow, dignified blink.

"Maybe it doesn't want to," she said. "It seems happy where it is."

"It has to come down," snapped the man. "I'm taking it to the vet."

"Why, what's wrong with it?"

"Cat flu. Hurry up, I don't have all day. Are you going to climb that tree or aren't you?"

He was behaving very strangely, Sam thought. Still, she'd offered to help him bring the cat down, so she'd better do it. Luckily she was pretty experienced at climbing trees, and this was an easy one, with plenty of footholds and branches to hang on to. From its perch above her, the cat watched her progress with interest.

At last she drew level with the branch where it sat. "Hello, cat," she said. "I'm here to rescue you. Although I'm not sure you need rescuing. Do you want to get down?"

The cat blinked lazily, as if to say it didn't really mind one way or the other.

Carefully, Sam reached out a hand to stroke its sleek, aristocratic head. The cat purred and rubbed against her hand. At least it was friendly. It could easily have spat at her and shot further up the tree.

"What's its name?" she called to the
man below.

"Its name? Er, Sofia."

"Sofia," she murmured, reaching out her hand. "Don't be scared, Sofia. I'm not going to hurt you."

"Yeowll," said the cat, as if it understood every word.

Sam picked it up carefully from the branch and held it close to her chest. With her free hand, she stroked its head, murmuring, "There, there. You really are the most beautiful cat. And you don't look at all sick. Do you really have the flu?"

"Yeowll," said the cat, which sounded to Sam like, "No, I don't!"

"What's happening?" the man called up. "Did you get it?"

Sam peered down at him through the branches. "Yes, I got it."

"So what's keeping you? You planning to spend all day up there?"

"Rude man," Sam muttered under her breath.

Keeping a firm hold on the cat she began to make her way down, but it wasn't so easy with only one free hand. Once she almost slipped and Sofia tightened her claws on Sam's shoulder.

"Don't worry," she murmured comfortingly. "You're safe."

At last she reached the ground. "Okay, give her to me," said the man in black.

But before she could hand Sofia over to him there came a shout from the house. "Stop! Stop, thief!"

At once the man turned and ran. He leaped over the wall with startling speed for someone with rheumatism and got into a car. Sam just had time to see a woman crouched over the steering wheel before the car took off with a squeal of brakes and drove down the road at high speed.

Chapter 2

A Really Exciting Assignment

Stunned, Sam stood holding the cat in her arms.

"Who are you?" A fair, plump woman in a purple outfit hurried towards her. "And what are you doing with my cat?"

"There, there was a man," Sam stammered. "He asked me to climb the tree and get the cat down. He, he said

17

he wanted to take it to the vet."

"To the vet indeed!" The woman snatched the cat out of Sam's arms and held it so tightly that it began to struggle. "And why should he want to take Sofia to the vet? There's nothing wrong with her."

"I, I didn't think there was," said Sam. "But why was he trying to get her down from the tree?"

"Because he's a thief. He keeps trying to steal my Sofia."

"Why? Is she valuable?" asked Sam.

"She is to me!" The woman held the cat against her cheek, murmuring, "Did the nasty man nearly get you this time, my precious? Don't worry, I won't let anyone take you away."

"Yeowll," said the cat.

"No wonder he seemed in such a

hurry," said Sam. "I bet he was afraid of being caught."

The woman sighed. "Oh, I can't tell you what a worry it is! I try to keep Sofia shut up indoors as much as possible, and I don't dare go out in case he breaks into the house."

"Why don't you tell the police?" asked Sam.

"Oh, the police wouldn't think it important enough. Besides, I can't ask them to stand guard over Sofia while I go shopping."

Sam had a brilliant idea.

"We could do that!" she said. "The Petsitters Club. We take care of other people's animals when they can't do it themselves. There are four of us: me, Matthew, Jovan, and Matthew's sister Katie. We'll stand guard over Sofia while you go shopping."

The woman looked doubtful. "You're very young."

"We're all experts," Sam assured her.

"Matthew and I are especially good with cats and dogs and Katie takes care of the creepy-crawlies. Oh, and Jovan's dad is Dr. Roy, the vet, so if an animal gets sick while we're looking after it, we can ask him for advice."

The woman still looked doubtful. "How much do you charge?"

"Nothing. We do it for our school's community service project. All you have to do is sign a form to say you're satisfied with the job we've done and then we get points for it. At the end of the semester the people who have the most points win a trophy." Sam reached out a hand to stroke the cat. "Sofia would be safe with us. We wouldn't let anyone steal her, especially that rude man. I wouldn't be fooled by him a second time!"

"Well, I do need to go to the stores,"

said the woman. Suddenly she seemed to make up her mind. "Could you possibly come this afternoon?"

"Yes, of course!" said Sam, delighted.

"My name is Mrs. Makepeace, by the way. See you at three o'clock."

Sam stopped by Matthew's house on the way home. She couldn't wait to tell him that this time they had a really exciting assignment: standing guard over a valuable cat to stop it from being stolen.

"You mean he's a cat burglar?" said Matthew.

"Sort of," said Sam.

Matthew looked worried. "Suppose he's dangerous? I think we should tell my dad."

Matthew and Katie's dad was a police officer.

"Mrs. Makepeace said it wasn't important enough to bother the police," said Sam. "Anyway I bet the four of us would be able to scare off any silly old cat burglar. You should have seen how fast he ran when he thought he was going to get caught! He even had a woman waiting for him in a getaway car."

Matthew still looked undecided. "What time do we have to be there?"

"Three o'clock, so we'd better meet at my house at two forty-five."

"Well, okay," he said at last. "I'll tell Katie at lunchtime. Can you stop by Dr. Roy's office on your way and tell Jo? I think he's helping his dad."

When Sam reached the vet's office, she found Jo outside in the garden, collecting pine cones.

"I thought you were supposed to be helping your dad," she said.

Jo looked embarrassed. "I said I'd wait outside. He has a really fierce hamster in there."

Sam was astonished. "I've never heard of a fierce hamster."

"You should see this one. It has teeth like a shark."

"Honestly, Jo. I sometimes wonder if you really *like* animals."

He shrugged awkwardly. "I like some of them," he mumbled. "The ones that don't bite."

"Sofia doesn't bite—and I should know, because she let me carry her down from the tree."

"Who's Sofia?"

Sam explained about the cat burglar. "See you at my house, Jo. Two forty-five. Don't be late."

"Okay," said Jovan, and went back to his pine cones.

Chapter 3

Keeping Watch

Sam told her father where they were going in case he noticed she was missing. Although he probably wouldn't have noticed, because he was busy in his den working on a cartoon. While she talked, he kept on drawing.

"So that's why Matthew and the others are coming over," she finished.

"Mmm," said Dad.

"And then we're all going to Mrs. Makepeace's house, to guard Sofia."

"Mmm," said Dad.

"She's the most beautiful cat you ever saw, smoky-gray with golden eyes. The cat burglar said she was Burmese."

"Mmm," said Dad.

The front doorbell rang.

Dad looked up from his drawing board. "Did you say cat burglar?"

"That's right," said Sam. She went to let the rest of the Petsitters Club into the house.

They filed into the den to say hello to Sam's father. Matthew entered first, followed by Jovan and finally Katie, clutching a small cardboard box.

"What's in the box?" asked Dad.

"Freddy and Freda," said Katie. "Roy Briggs asked me to look after them for him while he's away on vacation. I brought them along to teach them some tricks because I bet it could be a bit boring watching a cat."

"It may not be as boring as you think," said Sam. "Not if the cat burglar comes back."

"I told my dad about him," said Matthew. "He said if we had any trouble we should call the police station right away."

"I told my dad, too," said Jovan. "He said he knows Mrs. Makepeace and she doesn't have a cat."

"He must be thinking of someone else," said Sam.

Her father turned over a clean sheet of paper and began to draw.

Katie peered over the edge of the drawing board. "What's your cartoon about?" she asked him.

"You," he said.

Sam said to the others, "We'd better go or we'll be late. Bye, Dad."

"Bye, Petsitters."

Mrs. Makepeace was already wearing her hat and coat when they arrived. She took them into the kitchen to meet Sofia, who was reclining on a red cushion inside a wicker basket.

"There! I told you she was beautiful,"
Sam said to the others.

"Yeowll," said Sofia.

"Now, you will be careful, won't you?"
Mrs. Makepeace said, looking anxious.

"Keep all the windows shut and don't open the door to anyone. *Not anyone*, do you understand?"

"We understand," Matthew assured her.

Mrs. Makepeace glanced at the box in Katie's hands. "What's in there?"

"Freddy and Freda," said Katie. "I'm doing two petsitting jobs at the same time."

"Oh, I see." Mrs. Makepeace picked up her empty shopping bag. "Well, if you're sure . . . ?"

"We're sure," said Sam firmly.

"All I ask is that you don't leave Sofia alone for an instant. At least one of you must be with her at all times." She went to the front door. "I should be back in about an hour."

Sam put the chain on the door and went back to the kitchen. "So you see, your father was wrong," she said to Jovan. "She *does* have a cat. He must have forgotten."

Jovan glanced warily at Sofia. "A cat like that would be hard to forget."

"Yeowll," said Sofia.

They stood in a circle, staring down at her. Ignoring their presence, she began to wash her back leg with a long, pink tongue, taking care not to miss a single smoky-gray hair.

After a while, Katie grew fidgety. "I told you it would be boring. I'm going to teach Freddy and Freda some new tricks. It'll be a lot more fun than watching Sofia wash herself."

She placed the cardboard box on the table and took off the lid.

"There's a TV over there," said Jovan. "I don't think Mrs. Makepeace would mind if we turned it on."

"As long as we keep the sound turned down," said Sam. "It would be awful if the cat burglar broke in and we didn't hear."

Jovan turned on the television. He surfed the channels until he found an action adventure film and sat down to watch.

"It's stupid us all staying in here together," said Sam. "I'm going into the

front room. From there I'll have a good view of the road and the front path."

"Good idea," said Matthew. "And I'll look out from the kitchen window in case he tries to sneak around the back."

"Great," said Sam. "If that cat burglar comes back we have to be ready for him."

She went into the front room. The window had net curtains, which meant that she could look out without being

seen. She leaned her elbows on the windowsill and stared hard at the road.

Last time the cat burglar had come, he had had a car waiting for him outside, driven by a woman. The woman must have been his accomplice. They were probably a well-known cat-burgling gang.

The funny thing, now that Sam came to think about it, was that he had known Sofia's name. But then if he'd been trying

to steal her for some time, as Mrs. Makepeace said, no doubt he'd found out her name so that he could try to lure her away from the house. Only Sofia hadn't been fooled. She was a very aloof, intelligent type of cat, not at all the kind to let herself be kidnapped—or rather, catnapped—by a gang of thieves.

Sam yawned.

She was getting uncomfortable, standing up. If she sat on the sofa she would still be able to see out of the window. She sank into the cushions.

Aaah, much better. Before long she began to feel drowsy and found it hard to keep her eyes open.

Which was why she didn't hear a car drive up in the road outside.

Chapter 4

Katie's Circus

Jovan found it hard to concentrate on the action adventure film. It wasn't the same with the sound turned down. Silent car chases weren't nearly as exciting as noisy ones.

He glanced at Matthew, who had found a pair of binoculars and was using them to look out of the kitchen window. "Can you see anything?" he asked.

"Only a couple of birds fighting over a piece of bread," said Matthew.

Jovan sighed.

He glanced at Katie, who was getting more and more impatient with the inhabitants of the cardboard box because they wouldn't turn somersaults when she told them to.

"Oh, Freddy!" she groaned. "Come on, it's easy. Just hop over Freda and then land on my finger."

Who, or what, were Freddy and Freda anyway? As far as Jovan could see the box was empty. They were probably imaginary creatures, he thought. Little kids often made up things like that, or so he had heard. He didn't have any younger sisters himself, only an older brother who laughed at him because he was scared of animals.

He glanced at Sofia, who had finished washing her back leg and was now licking her paws. She seemed harmless enough, but he knew from experience that those velvety pads contained lethal weapons that she could unsheathe at any moment.

49

Sofia looked straight at him. "Yeowll," she said, and flexed her sharp little claws.

Chills ran up the back of Jovan's spine. It was almost as if she knew what he was thinking.

"Oh, no!" Katie wailed. "I've lost Freda."

Without looking around, Matthew said, "Then you'd better find her again, right?"

"Freda? Freda, where are you?" Katie began hunting under the table. "Oh, come on, Jo. Help me look."

Jovan sighed. "I would if I knew what I was looking for. But as Freddy and Freda seem to be invisible . . ."

"They're not invisible. They're just very, very small."

"What are they, anyway?"

"Fleas," said Katie.

There was a stunned silence.

Matthew swung around. "Did you say . . . *fleas?*"

"Yes," said Katie. "That's why I'm teaching them tricks, so they can be in Roy's circus."

"What kind of fleas?" Jovan demanded.

"Clever ones. Or at least, they're supposed to be. Actually, I think they're a bit stupid because they're no good at doing acrobatics."

"I meant are they *human* fleas?" he said. "Or are they *cat* fleas?"

"I didn't know there was any difference," Katie admitted.

Sofia sat up in her basket, looking alarmed. "Yeeowll!" she said.

"We'll soon find out what kind of fleas they are if she starts scratching," said Jovan.

"Or if *we* do," Matthew said grimly. "Honestly, Katie! You could have told

us what you were carrying around in that box."

Katie looked hurt. "You never asked. Oh, no! Now Freddy's escaped, too!"

"We'd better start looking for them," said Matthew. "Mrs. Makepeace isn't going to be very pleased if she comes back to find Sofia scratching like mad."

"The trouble with fleas is that they hop," Jovan pointed out. "They could be anywhere by now." He got down on his hands and knees to search the floor.

At that moment the doorbell rang.

Jovan went pale. "You don't think that's Mrs. Makepeace, back early?"

Matthew shook his head. "She wouldn't ring her own doorbell, would she? She'd have a key."

"Freddy? Freda?" called Katie, peering under the doormat. "Where are you?"

The doorbell rang again.

"That's funny," said Matthew. "Why doesn't Sam answer it?"

"I'll go," said Jovan. The truth was, he was glad to get out of the kitchen. All this talk about fleas was making him itch.

In the hall he met Sam, who came out of the front room rubbing her eyes. "Who is it?" she asked.

"I thought you'd know. Couldn't you see who it was from the window?"

"Er, no." She looked a bit embarrassed. "I think I must have fallen asleep."

The doorbell rang again, several times, as if the caller were getting impatient.

"I'd better answer it," said Sam.

"Be careful," Jovan warned. "It might be the cat burglar."

"Don't worry. I'll keep the chain on."

Chapter 5

Mrs. Dove

Sam opened the door as far as the chain would allow. Peering through the crack, she saw a fair, plump woman standing on the doorstep. For a moment she thought it was Mrs. Makepeace, but then she realized that the woman was wearing a red hat and she was certain that Mrs. Makepeace's hat had been green.

"Yes?" she said cautiously.

"Good afternoon," said the woman. "I've come to see my sister."

"I'm afraid she's out shopping," said Sam. "There's nobody here except us Petsitters."

"In that case, I'll come in and wait."

Sam hesitated. What if the woman wasn't Mrs. Makepeace's sister? What if she was the cat burglar's accomplice?

She tried to see over the woman's shoulder into the road. "Did you come by car?" she asked.

"Yes, of course. It's parked in the driveway." The woman pressed against the door. "Take off this chain, please."

Sam hesitated. "Mrs. Makepeace gave us strict instructions not to let *anyone* into the house."

"She was right. But I'm sure she didn't

mean me. After all, I am her sister."

Embarrassed, Sam asked, "Can you prove it?"

"Prove it? *Prove* it? What a strange thing to say! How can I possibly prove that I'm her sister?" The woman was clearly offended. "Except we do look a lot alike, or so people say."

"Yes, you do." Sam decided to take the risk. It seemed rude not to let the woman in. Besides, when Mrs. Makepeace came back, she might be angry with them for turning away her sister. She undid the safety chain and opened the door.

"Thank you." The woman stepped inside. "My name's Mrs. Dove, by the way."

"Mine's Sam, short for Samantha. And this is Jo."

"Pleased to meet you, Jo." Mrs. Dove looked around. "And where are the rest of the, er, Petsitters?"

"In the kitchen," Jo said. "But you'd better not go in there."

Too late. Mrs. Dove had already marched off down the hall.

Jovan caught Sam by the arm. "She can't go into the kitchen," he hissed. "It's not safe."

Sam stared at him. "What do you mean, it's not safe?"

"Freddy and Freda have escaped."

"So what?" She started to follow Mrs. Dove.

"You don't understand. They're . . ."

But Sam didn't wait to listen. She hurried to catch up with Mrs. Dove.

As they entered the kitchen, Matthew and Katie jumped up, looking guilty. Behind them on the table stood an empty cardboard box.

"Yeowll," said Sofia, and jumped out of her basket to greet Mrs. Dove.

"Ah, there you are, my angel!" Mrs. Dove bent down to pick up the cat. "Have you missed me? Are you glad to see me?"

Sofia purred like an engine, rubbing her head against Mrs. Dove's chin.

Sam relaxed. She had wanted proof that Mrs. Dove was Mrs. Makepeace's sister and here it was. Sofia obviously knew the visitor very well.

"Did Jo tell you that Freddy and Freda have escaped?" Katie asked her.

"Ssssh!" Matthew hissed at his sister.

"Yes, he did." Sam glanced at Jovan, who was standing in the doorway as if reluctant to come any further. Suddenly, to her astonishment, he did an impersonation of a monkey scratching itself. Was he trying to tell her something?

"Do you mind if I open a window?" asked Mrs. Dove. "It seems a little stuffy in here."

"No, we don't mind," said Sam, distracted by the strange way Jo was behaving.

Still holding Sofia, Mrs. Dove moved over to the window and opened it. "Ah, that's better!" She leaned right out, taking deep breaths of fresh air.

Suddenly, a pair of hands appeared out of nowhere, grabbed Sofia and disappeared again, leaving Mrs. Dove with empty arms.

Everyone was transfixed. "The cat burglar!" Sam exclaimed. "Quick, we can't let him get away!"

Chapter 6

Up a Tree—Again!

Sam burst out of the front door just in time to see the cat burglar, with Sofia in his arms, about to get into the car parked in the driveway. Not only had he stolen the cat, he was going to steal Mrs. Dove's car as well!

"Stop!" yelled Sam. "Stop, thief!"

The cat burglar wrenched open the

car door. As Sam raced towards him he started to slide into the driver's seat, and at that moment Sofia jumped out of his arms.

"Run, Sofia!" called Sam. "Run as fast as you can!"

Sofia streaked across the garden and shot up the same tree she had climbed before. The cat burglar chased after her, but stopped short at the foot of the tree. Sam arrived next, followed by the rest of the Petsitters.

Everyone stared up into the tree. Sofia crouched on a branch high above them, swishing her tail.

"Oh, my precious!" Mrs. Dove joined them, flushed and out of breath. "There's no need to be afraid. Come down to Mommy."

"Yeowll," said Sofia, glaring at the cat burglar.

"Horrible cat!" he exclaimed. "That's what she did before when I tried to get her, ran up the tree!"

"I'm not surprised," Sam said indignantly. "What do you expect if you go around grabbing cats out of windows? You frightened her half to death. Matthew, you'd better call your dad."

"Er, yes," said Matthew, backing away.

"His dad's a police officer," she told the cat burglar sternly.

He looked alarmed. "Now there's no need for that. After all, it's not as if I was trying to *steal* the horrible creature."

"Yes, you were!" Katie said accusingly. "We saw you."

"No, he wasn't," Mrs. Dove said unexpectedly. "This gentleman is my husband. He was only trying to get back my rightful property."

"What rightful property?" asked Jovan.

"My Sofia. She belongs to me, not my sister." Mrs. Dove peered up into the branches. "Come down, my sweetie, my angel."

Sam stared at her. "What do you mean, she belongs to you?"

"She's really my cat. My sister was only looking after her while we were away in New Zealand for three months, and now that we're back she won't give her up." Impatiently Mrs. Dove shook the tree. "Don't be silly, Sofia. Come to Mommy."

The cat burglar, who was really Mr. Dove, scratched his leg. "It's no use. She won't come down. You'll have to ask that girl to climb up and get her again."

Sam looked at the other Petsitters. They all looked back at her helplessly. This was a very difficult situation. Whom should they believe: Mrs. Makepeace or her sister?

Mr. Dove scratched his arm. "Go on, little girl. We'll make it worth your while."

"Yes, we will," said Mrs. Dove. "What did you say your name was? Sam, that's right, short for Samantha. Now Sam, if you climb up and get Sofia we'll give you some money. We'll give you *all* some money."

 "We're not allowed to take money," said Matthew. "We're doing this for our community service project."

"I suppose we could ask you to sign our form," Sam said doubtfully. "But how do we know you're telling the truth?"

Jovan cleared his throat. "My dad did say that Mrs. Makepeace didn't have a cat."

"There you are then!" said Mr. Dove triumphantly, scratching his leg again. "That *proves* we're telling the truth."

Still Sam hesitated. She didn't know what to think.

Then, to her relief, she saw Mrs. Makepeace hurrying through the front gate. "Here's your sister," she said. "You'd better sort it out between you."

"What's going on?" Mrs. Makepeace ran towards them. "Martha, have you been trying to steal Sofia again?"

Mrs. Dove looked furious. "No, Daisy, I have not! I'm simply trying to claim what is rightfully mine."

"She's not yours! You gave her to me."

"No, I certainly did *not* give her to you. I merely asked you to take care of her while we were away."

"You said you might not come back. You said you might stay in New Zealand forever. As far as I'm concerned, she's mine!"

"Well, I *did* come back. So she's mine!"

They glared at each other furiously.

Really, Sam thought, considering their names were Dove and Makepeace, the two sisters seemed very quarrelsome.

"Where is Sofia, anyway?" Mrs. Makepeace looked around the garden. "What have you done with her?"

"She's climbed up the tree again," said Mr. Dove, scratching his neck.

Mrs. Makepeace peered into the branches. "Oh, Sofia, there you are! Don't be afraid. I'm home now, so you can come on down."

"Yeowll," said Sofia, and jumped straight into Mrs. Makepeace's arms.

"You see?" said Mrs. Makepeace triumphantly. "*She* knows who her rightful owner is. She's my cat now."

Sam looked at Sofia, who was purring like an engine. The cat seemed as glad to see Mrs. Makepeace as she had previously been to see Mrs. Dove.

So who *was* the rightful owner of Sofia?

Chapter 7

Allergy!

"Now Martha, now Daisy," pleaded Mr. Dove. "I'm sure we can sort this all out if you'll only be reasonable. After all, it's only a cat." He scratched his elbow.

"Excuse me," said Katie, "but do you have an itch?"

"Er, yes . . . I do have a small one." He scratched his other elbow. "In fact I seem to be itching all over."

"Oh, good!" said Katie. "That means you've found . . ."

Matthew kicked her on the ankle. "It could be an allergy," he told Mr. Dove. "Maybe you're allergic to cats. A lot of people are."

Mrs. Dove looked annoyed. "He's never been allergic to them before."

"Well, I seem to be now," said her husband grumpily, trying to scratch his leg, his arm, and both elbows all at the same time.

"No, you're not," said Katie. "It just means . . ."

"An allergy can come on quite suddenly," Jovan interrupted. "My dad's always having to find new homes for cats whose owners have become allergic."

"Do you hear that, Martha?" Mr. Dove demanded. "I've developed an allergy to your confounded cat."

"No, you haven't!" shouted Katie, jumping up and down. *It just means you've found Freddy and Freda!*"

Mr. Dove stared at her. "Who are Freddy and Freda?"

"They're . . ." But before Katie could finish, Matthew clamped his hand over her mouth.

"Freddy and Freda are her imaginary friends," he said. "She gets a bit fanciful at times. You know what little kids are like."

Mr. Dove began to wriggle and jump around as if he was doing some kind of dance. "That settles it!" he told his wife. "I'm not having that cat back in our house if this is how it affects me. I never liked the horrible animal anyway."

Mrs. Dove turned pale. "You don't mean that?"

"Indeed I do. Either that cat stays here, or I move out!" Mr. Dove started dancing towards the car. "Hurry and make up your mind. This itch is driving me crazy!"

"Oh dear, oh dear." Mrs. Dove seemed torn with indecision.

"Of course, if we were friends again," Mrs. Makepeace told her sister, "you could come and visit Sofia and me as often as you like."

"Yes," said Mrs. Dove. "Yes, I suppose I could."

She glanced at her husband, who was already getting into the car. Suddenly she seemed to make up her mind.

"Okay, as long as I can see Sofia at least twice a week."

"You'll be welcome any time."

Sadly Mrs. Dove stroked Sofia's head. "Goodbye, my precious. Be a good girl for your Auntie Daisy. Mommy will come and see you often."

"Yeowll," said Sofia.

"Martha!" yelled Mr. Dove from the car. "Get a move on, can't you? I have to get away from here."

In silence, Mrs. Makepeace and the Petsitters watched Mr. and Mrs. Dove drive off down the road. When they had gone, Mrs. Makepeace said, "Oh, I can't tell you how relieved I am! Thank goodness everything has turned out for the best."

"Yes, it has," said Sam. "Please could you sign our form now?"

"Of course I will." She beamed at them all. "You've done an excellent job, Petsitters."

On the way home, Matthew said, "I'm glad Mrs. Makepeace got Sofia in the end, aren't you? I liked her better than Mr. and Mrs. Dove."

"So did I," Sam agreed. "Anyway, Mrs. Makepeace lives alone, so I bet she needs Sofia's company more than her sister does."

"I'm glad, too," said Jovan, "because Mrs. Dove kept saying 'Come to Mommy,' and I hate that. You should hear what my dad says about people who use baby talk to their animals."

Katie said nothing, but two large tears rolled down her cheeks.

"One thing confuses me," said Sam. "People who are allergic to cats don't usually itch all over. They sneeze a lot and their eyes run. I know, because my Aunt Cynthia's allergic. So why did Mr. Dove keep scratching himself?"

"Because he found Freddy and Freda, that's why." Matthew grinned. "At least we know now that they were human fleas and not cat fleas."

"*Fleas?*" Sam stared at him. Then she remembered Jovan doing his monkey impersonation and started to giggle. "No wonder they made him dance!"

Katie sniffed. "It's fine for you to laugh," she said sadly. "But what am I going to tell Roy Briggs? He'll be furious when he hears I lost his pets."

"Don't worry," said Jovan. "I'll ask my dad to find you a couple of fleas. I don't think Roy will be able to tell the difference."

"He will if they can't do tricks."

"You have plenty of time to teach them tricks," said Sam. "Roy won't be back from vacation for a week."

Katie brightened at once. "How soon can I have them, Jo?"

"We'll go over to the office now," said Jovan.

When Sam got home, she went into the den to find her father working hard at his drawing board.

"How did it go?" he asked.

"Well, it's a long story." She peered over his shoulder at the cartoon strip he was drawing. To her amazement, she saw herself and the rest of the Petsitters in Mrs. Makepeace's kitchen, and Mrs. Dove arriving, and Mr. Dove grabbing the cat out of the window, and even Mr. Dove dancing around in the garden, scratching himself.

"But that's *exactly* what happened!" she exclaimed. "How did you know?"

"I guessed," said Dad. "When you mentioned the cat burglar and Jo said that Mrs. Makepeace didn't have a cat, I could just imagine how the whole story would unfold."

"But, but how did you guess about the fleas?"

"I know Katie. And when she said that Freddy and Freda did tricks, it was pretty obvious that the creepy-crawlies in that cardboard box had to be fleas."

"Well, you could have warned us!" said Sam. "You'd have saved us a lot of trouble."

Dad grinned. "Ah, but that would have spoiled the fun, wouldn't it?"

And Sam had to agree with him.

The End

The **Petsitters Club** JOIN NOW!

You will receive:

- A membership certificate imprinted with your name!
- The official Petsitters Club newsletter sent to you four times a year
- A special "Members Only" Petsitters Club poster
- A Petsitters Club stuffed animal

Mail this coupon today to:
Barron's Educational Series, Inc., Dept. PC
250 Wireless Blvd., Hauppauge, NY 11788 • www.barronseduc.com

YES! I want to become a member of The Petsitters Club!

Please send my membership kit to:

Name _____

Address _____

City _____

State _____ Zip _____

Phone ( ) _____ Age _____

BARRON'S

Offer good in U.S. and Canada only.

Join The Petsitters Club for *more* animal adventures!

1. Jilly the Kid
3. Donkey Rescue
4. Snake Alarm!
5. Scruncher Goes Wandering
6. Trixie and the Cyber Pet